FIONA FRENCH won the 1986 Kate Greenaway Medal for her book
Snow White in New York. In 1992 *Anancy and Mr Dry-Bone*,
her first book for Frances Lincoln, was selected for Children's Books of the Year
and won the Sheffield Book Award. It was followed by Jill Paton Walsh's
Pepi and the Secret Names which was chosen as one of Child Education's Best Story
Books of 1994; *Lord of the Animals*; *Jamil's Clever Cat* and Joyce Dunbar's
The Glass Garden.
Her latest books are the stained-glass Bible stories
Bethlehem, Easter and *Paradise*.

For Janetta

The
Smallest
Samurai

A tale of Old Japan

Fiona French

F

FRANCES LINCOLN
CHILDREN'S BOOKS

Long ago in old Japan, Hana lived with her husband Tanjo in a small house near a temple. They both longed for a child.

One day Hana took gifts to the temple and laid them before the great Buddha.

"Please give me a child," she whispered, "even if it is only as big as a lotus flower."

A voice answered her. "Return home, Hana. Your wish has been granted."

Not long afterwards, Hana had a beautiful
baby boy.

"But he is so small!" she cried. "All the
neighbours will make fun of me."

She and Tanjo named the tiny boy Inchkin.
They took great care of him, but they did not
love him.

The years passed by, and Inchkin grew up to be clever and brave.

But he was still no bigger than a lotus flower and this made him sad, for he longed with all his heart to be like other men.

One day he said to his mother, "I will go out into the wide world to make my fortune, and maybe I will find a way to grow as tall as other people."

Making a sharp sword out of a needle and millet straw, and a strong suit of armour out of beetles' wings, Inchkin practised fighting crickets and bumblebees, and even a big mouse. He became a skilled swordsman.

One afternoon he climbed into a tiny boat made from a nutshell and sailed out on to the big river.

The swift-flowing tide took his boat through the city and beyond.

He had just reached the safety of a wide lake,
when a hand lifted him out of the water and
a voice high above him said, "Who are you?"
   "I am called Inchkin," he replied. "I am one of
the best swordsmen in Prince Sanjo's land."

"I *am* Prince Sanjo," said the voice. "So you must prove to me how good a swordsman you are."

Once ashore, Prince Sanjo set Inchkin down on the ground.

"Now, little warrior, I have a special task for you. My daughter is travelling to a temple far away in the mountains and you will guard her on her journey."

Inchkin bowed low, and took his place of honour in the princess's carriage.

Next day, when they arrived at the ancient temple, shadows were flitting among the trees.

Inchkin stood on the princess's shoulder to guard her more closely.

Suddenly two fiery demons who had strayed down from the mountains blocked their way.

The princess went pale, but Inchkin gripped his tiny sword, ready to defend her with his life.

"Come any closer and I will kill you!" he cried.

The two demons were astonished.

One of them loomed over him. "You are very frightening," he sneered. "Why, I could eat you in one mouthful!"

Inchkin lunged at him with his sharp sword.

"Aieee!" cried the demon.

Before the other demon knew what was going on, Inchkin leapt between them. Shouting a fierce battle-cry, he swung his sword in the air and stabbed him hard in the nose.

The demon howled with pain and both the evil spirits fled away.

At that moment the temple bells began
to ring and, as each pure note rang out across
the mountains, Inchkin felt himself grow
taller and taller. The Lord Buddha was
rewarding him for his bravery by granting
his dearest wish.

When the princess saw the handsome man,
her heart filled with joy.

Together they returned to the palace. Prince Sanjo gave them his blessing and the princess married her brave warrior.

So Inchkin became the greatest Samurai swordsman in the land, and they lived the rest of their lives in great happiness.

MORE TITLES BY FIONA FRENCH FROM FRANCES LINCOLN CHILDREN'S BOOKS

PARADISE

In seven days God created the universe, the world and its creatures.
They lived a perfect life in the Garden of Eden –
but one day, tempted by the serpent's seductive words,
Adam and Eve tasted the forbidden fruit of the tree of Knowledge.

ISBN 978-1-84507-092-2

JAMIL'S CLEVER CAT
A Folk Tale from Bengal

Sardul is the cleverest of cats. When he learns that his master,
Jamil the weaver, dreams of marrying a princess, he resolves to make
Jamil's wish come true. But how can he make Jamil appear
the richest man in the world, and so win the princess's hand?

ISBN 978-1-84507-518-7

LORD OF THE ANIMALS
A Native American Creation myth

Coyote has created the world and its creatures, and now he gathers
a council to decide how they will make the being who will rule over them all.
As the animals start to disagree, fur and feathers begin to fly –
until Coyote suggests they each make a clay model and then choose the best.
But, unknown to all of them, crafty Coyote has a plan of his own.

ISBN 978-0-71121-348-7

Frances Lincoln titles are available from all good bookshops.
You can also buy books and find out more about your favourite titles,
authors and illustrators on our website: www.franceslincoln.com